# Helping Hands

Written by Christine Ricci
Illustrated by Susan Hall

Louis Weber, C.E.O.
Publications International, Ltd.
7373 North Cicero Avenue, Lincolnwood, Illinois 60712
Ground Floor, 59 Gloucester Place, London W1U 8JJ

Customer Service: 1-800-595-8484 or customer_service@pilbooks.com

www.pilbooks.com

Manufactured in China.

p i kids is a registered trademark of Publications International, Ltd.

8 7 6 5 4 3 2 1

ISBN-13: 978-1-4127-8921-9
ISBN-10: 1-4127-8921-4

 publications international, ltd.

¡Hola! I'm Dora and this is my best friend, Boots. I hear someone crying. Do you see anyone who might need help? It's a little duck! Little Duck says that she's lost.

Don't worry, Little Duck. We can help you! Little Duck lives on a farm. But we don't know how to get to the farm. Who do we ask for help when we don't know which way to go? Map!

Map says that to get to the Farm, first we need to go through Butterfly Forest and then go across the Windy River. First we need to find Butterfly Forest. Do you see it? Let's go!

I hear a "WHOOOO" sound. Who's making that sound? It's our friend the owl, La Lechuza. La Lechuza is stuck in a net. We can help her! Will you check my Backpack for safety scissors?

The safety scissors cut the net and La Lechuza is safe! We've got to keep going to get Little Duck home. La Lechuza is showing us the way to Butterfly Forest. Which path is La Lechuza pointing to? Great! We'll take the green path!

We made it to Butterfly Forest.
Oh no! A baby tapir is stuck in a mud puddle.
C'mon, let's help him! Alright! We helped the
baby tapir get out of the mud! Mommy Tapir
is so happy that her baby is safe.

Next we need to find the Windy River. Do you see a river? There it is! And I see a boat! Let's go!

Whoa! This Windy River sure is windy! The wind is making lots of waves in the river! Which wave is the biggest? Oh no! That big wave is headed right for the turtle family.

We've got to help them! We need something that we can use to rescue the turtles. Let's check Backpack!

Our life preserver saved the turtle family from that big wave. All the turtles are safe! Now we just need to help Little Duck find her farm. Do you see a farm? There it is!

We did it! Little Duck is back home with her family. It makes me feel great to have helped so many friends! You are a great helper! We couldn't have done it without you!